Space Baby

First published in Great Britain 1998 by Heinemann Young Books
an imprint of Reed International Books Limited.
Michelin House, 81 Fulham Rd, London SW3 6RB
Published in hardback by Heinemann Educational Publishers,
a division of Reed Educational and Professional Publishing Limited
by arrangement with Reed International Books Limited.
Text copyright © Annie Dalton 1998
Illustrations copyright © David Axtell 1998
The Author and Illustrator have asserted their moral rights
Paperback ISBN 0 7497 3131 1
Hardback ISBN 0 434 80064 3
10 9 8 7 6 5 4 3 2 1
A CIP catalogue record for this title is available from the British Library
Printed at Oriental Press Limited, Dubai

ANNIE DALTON

Space Baby

ILLUSTRATED BY DAVID AXTELL

 YELLOW BANANAS

For
Rae, Ricardo and Pia
and their father Kevin Percival
and
for Diane Browne
who started me thinking.

Chapter One

THE DAY DAD told us he had to go away, my brother Tee slammed out of the house and my little sister Riley ran upstairs crying.

And Dad said sadly, 'Cameron, look after everyone for me while I'm gone.'

So I promised. But it felt scary. It felt wrong. Because Tee's the oldest. Tee's the best at everything, not me.

He's got a star map with all the names. He used to say space scientists were going to discover a new world one day. 'Where there's no dirty concrete,' he said. 'And where people look after trees and rivers and are kind to each other.'

Tee always watched the news, to see if anyone had found that world yet.

Then one day Tee got tired of waiting. He said space stuff was only for sad little kids like me.

Now Dad's gone, all Tee does is hang around with Jankro's gang. Sometimes, when he's late home and Riley has her bad dreams, I unfold his old star map and read the names aloud to her, one by one, till she falls asleep again. After all, I did promise Dad I'd look after her.

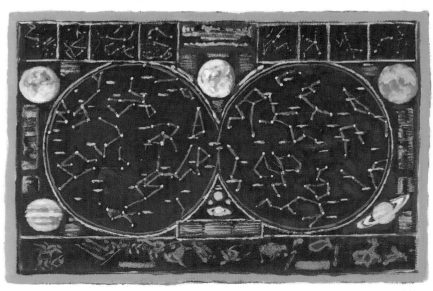

One afternoon I was late leaving school. Someone had pinched my trainers. By the time I gave up looking it was dark and raining in buckets.

I almost took the short cut home past the junkyard, but that's Jankro's territory. So I went the long way.

When I walked into the kitchen the smell of burnt food made me cough. Gran was scrubbing a pan.

'What happened, Gran?'

'I let the rice boil dry,' she said crossly. 'We don't have one grain of rice left. I told Riley I'd fry up some dumplings but she wants my special rice.'

Riley is babyish lately. But she's right about the rice. I can't imagine Gran's fried chicken without it.

So I said, 'I'll fetch some.'

But my heart started thumping. Our corner shop is in Jankro's territory. I might run into his gang. Wind and rain wouldn't keep them off the street. The only weather they care about is the weather of pure wickedness.

Riley came after me, looking like a weird little goblin, wearing one of Dad's old jumpers and his woolly hat. She often wears his things now.

'I want to spend my money,' she whined.

'All right, keep your hair on,' I told her.

The street lights mostly don't work round our way. We ran through the dark patches and slowed down in the light ones.

Suddenly Riley yanked my arm. 'Look at that star!' she yelled, pointing at a brilliant light, breaking through the clouds. It seemed to be shining straight at us.

'When they're that bright, they're planets,' I told her. It was so close you could see swirly colours in it. 'It's a beautiful new world,' I told her. 'One day we'll go there.'

'Who lives on it?' asked Riley doubtfully.

'Only kind people,' I said. That cheered her up. She was singing by the time we reached the shop! And we didn't see Jankro's gang anywhere.

Riley took ages choosing. My head was still full of swirly colours. I felt dreamy, as

if nothing bad could
happen now. A big mistake.
Gran says wickedness never sleeps.

So after Riley stuffed her pockets
with those stupid love hearts she always
buys, I said, 'Let's take the short cut.'

'Okay,' said my sister. And she stomped
down the dark lane towards the junkyard,
singing her weird little song, with Dad's
hat slipping over her eyes.

And then the dazzling light from
the sky came hurtling straight at us.

Chapter Two

THE SKY WAS raining fizzy colours. It rained sounds too. It sounded like singing, only without any words.

'Did the planet blow up?' Riley whimpered, rubbing her eyes.

'Maybe it wasn't a planet,' I said. 'Maybe something crashed.'

'You mean a plane?' said Riley amazed.

'No, a space ship,' I shouted, starting to run. 'Over there in the junkyard. You'll have to help me through the wire!'

'I'm coming too,' said my sister.

We scrambled through a gap. At once the air filled with wolfish howls. I'd forgotten those crazy junkyard dogs.

'Go back, Riley,' I yelled.

'No,' she screamed. 'I want to see the kind star people.'

So we ran on together into the light. The strange singing got louder. Then it spluttered out, lights, singing, everything. And we were alone.

'But it landed here,' I whispered.

'Cam,' said Riley, pointing into the sky. 'Is that a space ship?'

My heart nearly stopped. I wanted to cry. A real space ship at last and Tee was missing it.

But the craft was already speeding away.
Soon it looked like just another far-off star.

'So why did it land?' asked Riley, shivering.

'Maybe it left something behind. Something
precious,' I told her. 'Maybe the star people
chose us to keep it safe, until they come back
again.' I was surprised to hear myself say that.

But when we found the 'something' it didn't
look like much. It looked like, well,
something you'd find in a junkyard. A dull,
egg-shaped thing, the size of a small cement
mixer.

At that exact
same moment
the dogs came
panting up. I
grabbed a lump
of wood but
suddenly a sweet
bell-like sound
started up. The
dogs backed
away, whining.

'Oh-oh, it's the egg,' said Riley. 'Something's happening!'

Gently the egg unfolded itself, petal by petal, like a gigantic sunflower. At last thirteen petals were curled back, gold and shining.

The dogs made shocked whining noises down their noses.

I couldn't move.

'Ohhh, Cameron!' breathed Riley.

Inside the sunflower was a sleeping baby. She was gold too, golden as a plum. Even the wispy twists of her hair were a fiery gold.

'She's got no clothes,' said Riley.

Suddenly we heard big boots crashing through the dark, kicking bits of old car and rusty washing machine out of their way.

'What if they've got lasers?' someone yelled in a husky voice. 'What if they've got germ warfare?'

'What do you care? Think how much the Government will pay to get hold of it,' said someone else, in a voice colder than outer space.

That was Jankro. The husky one was Snake.

If Jankro found the baby he'd hand her over to the Government too. I picked her up, buttoning my jacket over her to keep her

warm. I could feel her tiny heart beating, like
a bird's.

'Quick, run!' I hissed. We ran so fast Riley's
hat blew off, but I wouldn't let her stop and
pick it up.

I looked back. The dogs were growling again, baring their teeth. Snake kicked them away.

'This is solid gold, man!' he shouted. Then he yelled hoarsely, 'Tee, get over here and look at this!'

Our big brother Tee was in the junkyard too!

I grabbed Riley's hand then and we didn't stop running until we were safe inside Gran's kitchen.

Chapter Three

'WHAT IN THE world . . . ?' Gran said when she saw what was peeping out of my jacket.

'It's a baby,' I gasped.

The space baby was awake. Her eyes were a dark greenish gold, like the river in summer, but with a far-off light in them.

'La la,' she sang, unafraid. Her small voice was strangely comforting. Gran's kitchen suddenly seemed warmer and brighter.

'I can see what it is,' snapped Gran. 'But what kind?' She took the golden baby from my arms. Gran loves little children, whatever planet they're from.

'La, la,' the baby sang. And she patted Gran's cheek and laughed.

'She's a girl,' said Riley. 'We found her. Can she be my sister?'

Gran shook her head. 'This one is no ordinary child.'

I couldn't believe it! I thought it was going to be murder explaining a space baby. But Gran knew everything already!

'Eh-eh,' Gran said sighing, 'the Heavenly Host must be having some troubled times if they can't keep track of their own angels. What do they call those little ones? Cherubs?'

'Er yes,' I said. 'Cherubs. But Gran . . .'

'Poor mite,' said Gran, stroking the baby's golden spine. 'Her wings haven't even grown yet.'

I gave up. If Gran believed the baby was an angel, so much the better.

'Gran, we've got to keep her a secret,' I said.

'Because I've got this white hair sprouting out of my head, you think I'm a fool, boy?' said Gran. 'You think I'd trust any old somebody with this little one?'

'I meant, you can't tell Tee,' I said, awkwardly.

Gran put her chin in the air, like a warrior queen. 'I know what you meant,' she said.

But her eyes were sad.

She sent Riley upstairs to find some old baby clothes and made me set the pan on the stove to cook the rice.

Then Gran fetched a drawer for a cradle and carefully lined it with a cut-up quilt. And I fed milky cereal to our new sister. She swallowed every spoonful, even though it was earth food.

We put her to sleep in Riley's room.

Later that night I was woken by the wail of police cars. It was pitch dark. Tee's bed was still empty.

I peeped into Riley's room.

'Cam,' Riley whispered. 'I thought she might be lonely so I let her share my bed. She's talking to some sweet little lights, look!'

I tiptoed in.

Tiny coloured lights were zipping about in the darkness, like fireflies.

Sometimes the lights joined up and turned into dazzling writing, but the words moved too fast to read. Anyway I don't think they were written in earth language. Some of the writing zoomed up through the ceiling. The rest disappeared through the floor.

'La la la,' sang the baby, waving her hands. And new shoals of gold and silver scribbles swam out through the walls into the street.

'She's doing that, Riley,' I said, amazed. 'The light goes where she sends it.'

I started shivering. It had been a long strange day.

Riley pulled back her covers and threw out her biggest teddy to make room. 'Get in, Cam,' she offered.

So my sister and I lay watching as the space baby filled the sleeping city with dazzling messages from another world. The room began to feel crowded in a kind of zingy, tingly way. It was hard to keep my eyes open.

As I slid into sleep I thought: 'Now everything is going to change.'

And I felt sad because Tee wasn't with me
to see it.

Chapter Four

BUT IN THE morning everything was exactly the same. The leak on the stairs was still there. So was that sinister mould near the wash basin which makes Riley scared to brush her teeth.

Gran said we had to go to school as usual.

'But the baby . . .' I argued.

'You think I can't look after babies!' Gran glared. Then she softened. 'If we don't want folk to be suspicious, we must carry on as normal.'

But as it turned out, my day wasn't normal at all. In fact, it was so extraordinary, I couldn't wait to find out if Riley's was as weird as mine.

I was shouting before I opened the back door. 'Can you believe it! I climbed the ropes just like Tarzan. Then we wrote a story. I wrote two pages without stopping. Miss Sheridan said it was the best story she'd ever read,' I yelled, helping myself to an apple.

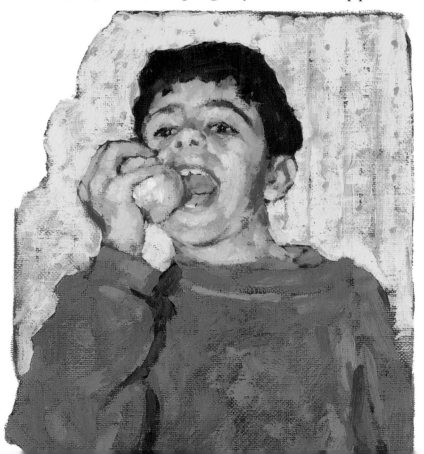

'She said it sounded just like me, so it must have been me, even if the star people helped.'

I went into the sitting room, munching. Then my heart turned over.

Tee was sprawled on the sofa. He had purple bruises over his eye and a nasty gash under one ear. He looked like a mean ugly stranger.

'Sit down, Cam,' he said, patting the cushion. 'Had a busy day?'

'I'm not telling you nothing,' I shouted. 'You used to be a brilliant brother, but now you're just a – a stupid gangster like Jankro.'

Tee grabbed my arm, twisting it hard. 'Big words,' he said. 'Going to back them up with your fists, little brother?'

Tears of pain squeezed from my eyes. 'If I have to.'

Suddenly Tee let go and covered his face. 'Cam, I don't want this crazy life any more.' A tear splashed on his trainers. 'I want it how it was when Dad was here.'

'Me and Riley didn't go away,' I said stonily. 'Nor did Gran.'

Tee looked ashamed. Then he pulled Dad's hat out of his pocket. 'I picked this up in the junkyard. I saw you last night.'

I went a bit crazy then. 'You're not having our space baby!' I yelled. 'Not if you twist my arm right off! Snake thinks that golden egg is such a big deal but the baby's the true treasure. All the gold in the world couldn't buy her.'

Tee looked deadly tired. 'If Jankro knew what you've stolen from under his nose, he'd take her back and he wouldn't care how.' He winced with pain. His sleeve was torn and bloodstained.

'Did they do that to you?' I asked, horrified.

He tried to grin. 'You should see Snake.'

'You fought Snake? Why?'

'To give you time to get away,' said Tee. 'To stop them seeing you and following you. Then I circled the streets till it was safe to come back.'

Tee had known about the baby all the time! He'd spent the night alone on the streets to keep Jankro's gang away from our house. I didn't know what to say.

'Can I see that little space baby, man?' said Tee softly. 'Where is she?'

'Gran and Riley have probably taken her somewhere,' I said.

'They left in a big hurry then,' said Tee. 'The door was wide open when I got here and their coats are still hanging up.'

I hit myself hard. 'Tee, I think Jankro's got them!'

I wrenched open the front door and ran into the street. Tee struggled after me. But there was no sign of a space baby, a weird little sister or a fierce warrior Gran.

But there was something. A love heart in the gutter. It said, ANGEL FACE.

Chapter Five

THE NEXT SWEET said DON'T BE SHY. Then Tee spotted SAY YES. I found SMILE and TRUST ME.

'This is like Hansel and Gretel in the forest,' I said.

We were running like mad now.

'Hansel and what?'

'You read me that story, Tee,' I panted. 'You don't fool me.'

'Well now I'm in the big bad world all by myself,' scowled Tee.

'So were Hansel and Gretel,' I said, crawling

through the wire into the junkyard.

Tee cuffed my ear. 'You've got a smart mouth.'

But the trail of sweets had fizzled out.

Then, behind toppling rusty castles of junk, we heard her.

'La la,' she sang, unafraid. 'La la la.'

We heard something else too. Big daft dogs sighing down their noses like lonely puppies.

'She's not an ordinary baby, Snake,' I heard Riley explain. 'She does star magic. It makes the dogs be gentle.'

I can't describe how Tee looked then. But something changed in his eyes and I knew he wasn't a gangster any more.

Snake did his husky laugh. 'Magic! The kid's not old enough to hold a spoon.'

'Clarence Hillman,' rapped Gran's voice. 'If you'd paid attention in Sunday School, you'd recognise an angel when you met one. There's nothing angels can't do when they've a mind. Tame lions, walk through the fire . . .'

'Clarence,' spluttered Tee. I've got to see this.'

We peered around a skip overflowing with old tyres. There was Jankro and that boy Sugar who thinks he's so cool with his yellow cap. The rest of Jankro's gang were standing

around Gran and Riley like hungry wolves. I clenched my fists. If Tee and I had to fight to save the space baby, that's what we'd do.

Then I saw Snake. I hardly recognised him. His face looked so terrible after his fight with Tee. On top of everything it was hot with shame.

He tossed his head. 'The name's 'Snake',
Grandma.'

'My rheumatism hasn't twinged
once since that little baby
came to live with us,' Gran
went on.

'Can't you hear me?' Jankro

yelled down his mobile phone. 'This is a live alien I'm talking about. Well, baby size at the moment. But she's already got super powers.

She tames savage beasts. Hello? Hello?'

Then the baby moved her hands again, singing her wordless song, and something amazing happened.

The whole world rearranged itself inside me. Suddenly I saw, not the way things looked, but the way they really were.

I looked at Jankro's wicked wolves and saw a bunch of scared kids wearing giant sized basketball boots. Kids like Tee who'd got tired of waiting. One day they'd stopped dreaming and started hustling for money instead.

The junk looked different too. Instead of being ugly trash no one loved or wanted, you could see it was burning to be changed and used for something wonderful and new.

'Imagine what you could make with some of this,' Tee whispered.

'There's no angels any more, Grandma,' Sugar said sullenly.

'La la la,' sang the baby, laughing.

'She's just . . .' Sugar ducked a second too late. Stars skimmed across his cap like tiny frisbees '. . . an alien?' he squeaked, backing away.

Jankro collapsed on an old car. All the fight had gone out of him. 'I can't believe those government fools,' he muttered. 'We could have done a deal, man, but instead they treated me like - rubbish.' He aimed a kick at the burnt out car.

'Go on, have my last one,' Riley said gently, pushing a love heart into his hand.

Jankro looked down at the sweet in astonishment. 'What's this meant to be?'

A bubble of laughter rose up in my throat. There was nothing to be scared of now. I ran out and hugged Gran. Tee followed, bruised, bloodstained and shy.

'What have I always told you about fighting, boy?' Gran scolded.

'Sorry, Gran,' said Tee.

The baby touched him with delicate fingers.

'What's she doing?' Tee said trembling.

'Mending your poor face,' said Riley.

'This is your new sister,' said Gran.

Tee stroked the baby's soft twists of hair.

'La la,' she sang lovingly.

Jankro was still staring at Riley's last love heart.

'I'll read it, shall I?' said my sister bossily. 'It says BE KIND. So now you'll always be kind, won't you?'

Jankro made choking sounds.

'We'll head home,' said Gran firmly. 'If you've finished, boys?'

The street lights were flickering on as the five of us walked home, Gran, Tee, the baby, Riley and me.

'After tea,' said Riley sweetly, slipping her hand into mine. 'You can take me to the shop.' Her feet were making slithery clumping sounds.

'Are those Dad's shoes you're wearing, you little weirdo?' I demanded. 'Anyway you spent all your money last night.'

'That's not fair. I gave my hearts to save the baby,' she moaned.

'Keep your hair on,' said Tee. 'If you put some sensible shoes on, I'll take you. Is that a deal?'

'It's a deal,' giggled Riley, smacking Tee's palm with hers.

And my goblin sister went slithering and clumping ahead of us, singing her little out of tune song, all the rest of the way home.

Yellow Bananas are bright, funny, brilliantly imaginative stories written by some of today's top writers. All the books are beautifully illustrated in full colour.

So if you've enjoyed this story, why not pick another one from the bunch?

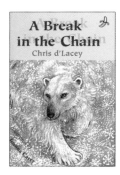